1

THIS WALKER BOOK BELONGS TO:

_____

_____

_____

_____

For Liz
S.H.

For Jill
T.G.

ACKNOWLEDGEMENTS

Every effort has been made to trace the ownership of all
copyrighted material and to secure the necessary permissions
to reprint these selections. In the event of any questions
arising as to the use of any material, the editor and the
publisher, while expressing regret for any inadvertent error,
will be happy to make the necessary correction in future printings.

Grateful acknowledgement is made to the following for
permission to reprint the copyrighted material listed below:

A & C Black (Publishers) Ltd in association with Inter-Action
Inprint for the first verse of "The Monster Stomp" by John Perry
from GAME-SONGS WITH PROF DOGG'S TROUPE. "I'm a Little Robot"
collected by Linda Friend from OKKI-TOKKI-UNGA.
Reproduced by permission of A & C Black (Publishers) Ltd.

Hamish Hamilton Ltd for "One-Eyed Jack"
from MOTHER GOOSE LOST by Nicholas Tucker.

First published 1988 by Walker Books Ltd
87 Vauxhall Walk, London SE11 5HJ

This edition published 1989
Reprinted 1990, 1991, 1992 (twice)

This selection © 1988 Sarah Hayes
Illustrations © 1988 Toni Goffe

Printed and bound in Hong Kong by
Sheck Wah Tong Printing Press Ltd

British Library Cataloguing in Publication Data
Stamp your feet: action rhymes.
1. Nursery rhymes in English – Anthologies.
I. Hayes, Sarah   II. Goffe, Toni
398'.8
ISBN 0-7445-1232-8

STAMP YOUR FEET
ACTION RHYMES

Chosen by Sarah Hayes   *Illustrated by* Toni Goffe

CONTENTS

The Monster Stomp ... 6

Can You Walk on Tip-toe ... 7

Peter Hammers ... 8

The Wheels on the Bus ... 10

Down by the Station ... 12

I'm a Little Robot ... 13

Row Your Boat ... 13

Old John Muddlecombe ... 14

Hickory Dickory Dock ... 15

I'm a Little Teapot ... 16

Hippety-Hop ... 16

Currant Buns ... 17

Rain ... 18

White Sheep ... 19

Ring-a-Ring o' Roses ... 20

Pitter-Patter Raindrops ... 21

One-Eyed Jack ... 22

One Elephant ... 24

The Farmer's in His Den ... 26

Miss Polly ... 28

WALKER BOOKS
LONDON

THE MONSTER STOMP

If you want to be a monster, now's your chance
'Cause everybody's doing the monster dance,

You just stamp your feet,   Wave your arms around,

Stretch 'em up, stretch 'em up,   Then put them on the ground,
'Cause you're doing the monster stomp
That's right, you're doing the monster stomp.
Ooh-Ah-Ooh-Ah-Ooh-Ah-Ooh-Ah
Ooh-Ah-Ooh-Ah-Ooh-Ah-Ooh-Ah

CAN YOU WALK ON TIP-TOE

Can you walk on tip-toe
As softly as a cat?

And can you stamp
along the road,
Stamp, stamp, just like that?

Can you take some
great big strides
Just like a giant can?

Or walk along so slowly
Like a poor bent old man?

PETER HAMMERS

Peter hammers with one hammer,
One hammer, one hammer.
Peter hammers with one hammer
All day long.

Peter hammers with two hammers,
Two hammers, two hammers.
Peter hammers with two hammers
All day long.

Peter hammers with three hammers,
Three hammers, three hammers.
Peter hammers with three hammers
All day long.

Peter hammers with four hammers,
Four hammers, four hammers.
Peter hammers with four hammers
All day long.

Peter hammers with five hammers,
Five hammers, five hammers.
Peter hammers with five hammers
All day long.

Peter's going to sleep now,
Sleep now, sleep now.
Peter's going to sleep now
All day long.

PETER'S WIDE AWAKE NOW,
AWAKE NOW, AWAKE NOW.
PETER'S WIDE AWAKE NOW
ALL DAY LONG.

THE WHEELS ON THE BUS

The wheels on the bus go round and round,
Round and round, round and round,
The wheels on the bus go round and round,
All day long.

The grans on the bus
go knit, knit,
knit...

The children on the bus
go wriggle, wriggle,
wriggle...

The dads
on the bus
go nod, nod,
nod…

The mums
on the bus
go chatter, chatter,
chatter…

The wipers
on the bus
go swish, swish,
swish…

The horn on the bus
goes beep, beep,
beep…

The driver on the bus
goes bother, bother,
bother…

DOWN BY THE STATION

Down by the station,
early in the morning,
See the little puffer trains,
all in a row.

See the engine driver
pull the little handle.

Toot toot, puff puff,
off we go!

I'M A LITTLE ROBOT

I'm a little robot,
short and square,

I have no toenails,
I have no hair.

When you want the answer to your sums,
Just press my button and out it comes.

ROW YOUR BOAT

Row, row, row your boat,
Gently down the stream.
Merrily, merrily, merrily, merrily,
Life is but a dream.

OLD JOHN MUDDLECOMBE

Old John Muddlecombe
Lost his cap.

He couldn't find it
anywhere,
Poor old chap.

He walked down the street,
And everybody said:

"Silly John Muddlecombe,
You've got it on your head!"

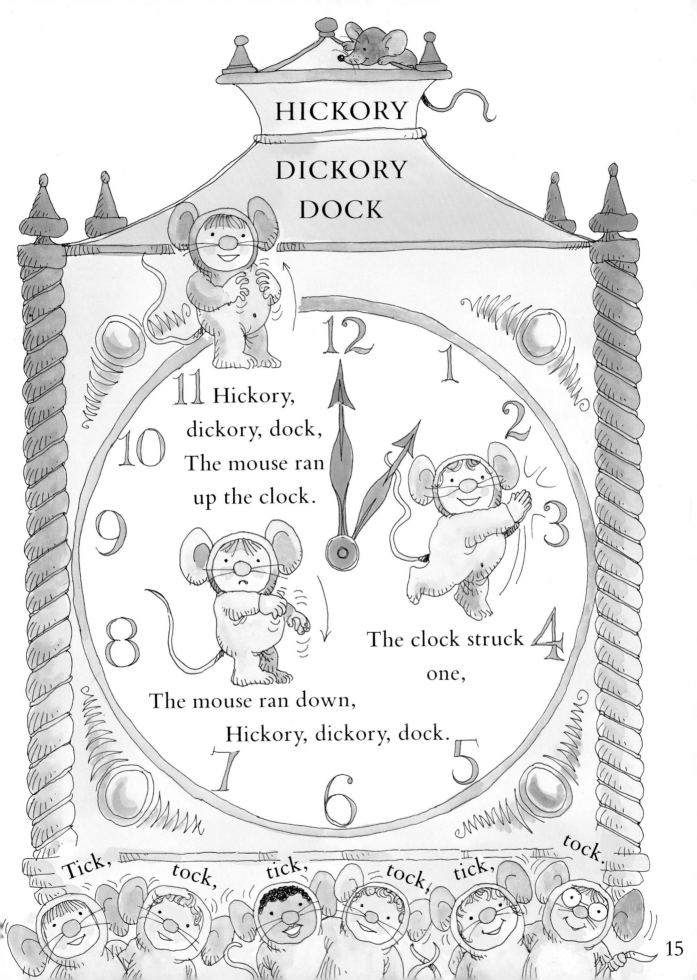

HICKORY

DICKORY

DOCK

Hickory,
dickory, dock,
The mouse ran
up the clock.

The clock struck
one,

The mouse ran down,
Hickory, dickory, dock.

Tick, tock, tick, tock, tick, tock.

15

I'M A LITTLE TEAPOT

I'm a little teapot,
  short and stout;
Here's my handle,
  here's my spout.

When the water's boiling,
  hear me shout:
"Just tip me over and
  pour me out."

HIPPETY-HOP

Hippety-hop to the baker's shop, to buy three sticks of candy.

One for you,   and one for me,   and one for sister Sandy.

CURRANT BUNS

Five currant buns in a baker's shop,
Round and fat with a cherry on the top.

Along came a boy with a penny one day,
He bought a currant bun,

And he took it away.
Four currant buns in a baker's shop…

RAIN

Rain on the house-tops,

Rain on the tree,

Rain on the green grass—

But don't rain on me!

18

WHITE SHEEP

White sheep, white sheep
On a blue hill,

When the wind stops
You all stand still.

You all run away
When the wind blows,

White sheep, white sheep
Where do you go?

RING-A-RING O' ROSES

Ring-a-ring o' roses,
A pocket full of posies,

A-tishoo, a-tishoo!
We all fall down.

PITTER-PATTER RAINDROPS

I hear thunder, I hear thunder.
So do I, so do I.

Pitter-patter raindrops,
pitter-patter raindrops,
I'm all dry.
So am I.

I hear thunder, I hear thunder.
Hark, don't you, hark, don't you?

Pitter-patter raindrops,
pitter-patter raindrops,
I'm wet through.

So are you –   and you –

and you!

ONE-EYED JACK

One-eyed Jack,
the pirate chief,
Was a terrible,
fearsome ocean thief.

He wore a peg
Upon one leg.

One-eyed Jack,
the pirate chief,
A terrible, fearsome
ocean thief.

He wore a hook
And a dirty look.

ONE ELEPHANT

One elephant went out to play
Upon a spider's web one day.
He thought it such a tremendous stunt
That he called for another little elephant.

Two elephants went out to play
Upon a spider's web one day.
They thought it such a tremendous stunt
That they called for another little elephant.

Three elephants went out to play
Upon a spider's web one day.
The web went CREAK
The web went CRACK
And all of a sudden
They all ran back.

THE FARMER'S IN HIS DEN

The farmer's in his den,
The farmer's in his den,
Ee-i the derry-o
The farmer's in his den.

The farmer wants a wife,
The farmer wants a wife,
Ee-i the derry-o
The farmer wants a wife.

The wife wants a child,
The wife wants a child,
Ee-i the derry-o
The wife wants a child.

The child wants a nurse,
The child wants a nurse,
Ee-i the derry-o
The child wants a nurse.

The nurse wants a dog,
The nurse wants a dog,
Ee-i the derry-o
The nurse wants a dog.

The dog wants a bone,
The dog wants a bone,
Ee-i the derry-o
The dog wants a bone.

We all pat the dog,
We all pat the dog,
Ee-i the derry-o
We all pat the dog.

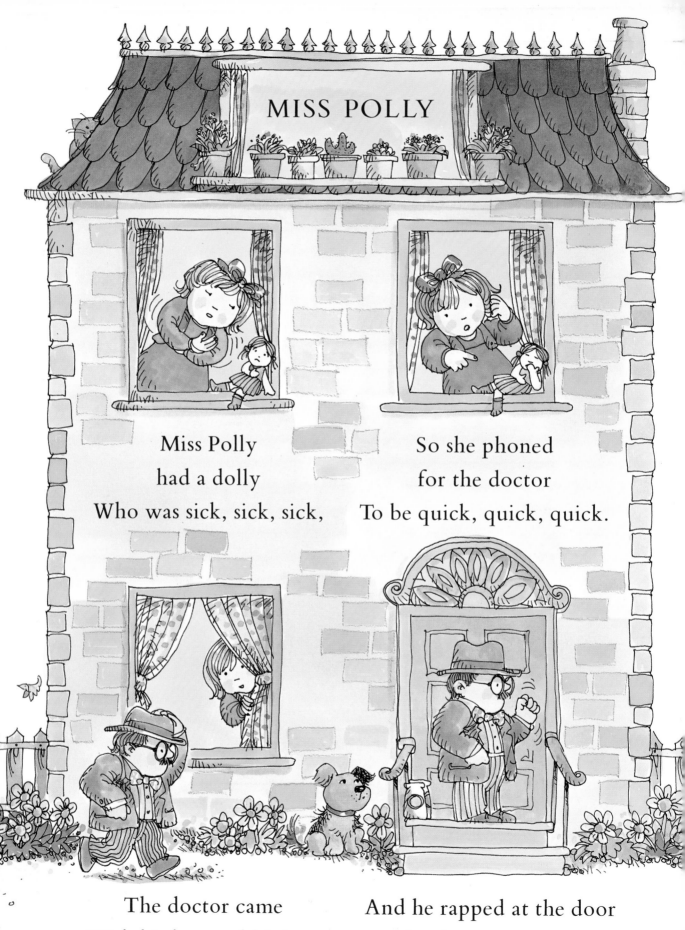

MISS POLLY

Miss Polly
had a dolly
Who was sick, sick, sick,

So she phoned
for the doctor
To be quick, quick, quick.

The doctor came
With his bag and his hat,

And he rapped at the door
With a rat-tat-tat.

He looked
at the dolly
And he shook his head.

Then he said,
"Miss Polly,
Put her straight to bed."

He wrote on a paper
For a pill, pill, pill.

"I'll be back in the morning
With my bill, bill, bill."

29

MORE WALKER PAPERBACKS
For You to Enjoy

Also by Sarah Hayes

CLAP YOUR HANDS
illustrated by Toni Goffe

A second rousing collection of Action Rhymes.
"Jolly rhymes… Lively, friendly illustrations." *Books for Keeps*
ISBN 0-7445-1231-X   £3.99

THIS IS THE BEAR
THIS IS THE BEAR AND THE PICNIC LUNCH
illustrated by Helen Craig

Two rollicking cumulative rhymes about a boy, a dog and a bear.
"For those ready for their first story, there could be no better choice…
Helen Craig's pictures are just right." *Judy Taylor, The Independent*

This Is the Bear   0-7445-0969-6
This Is the Bear and the Picnic Lunch   0-7445-1304-9
£3.99 each

BAD EGG
illustrated by Charlotte Voake

The true story of Humpty Dumpty.
"Entertaining gloss on a traditional rhyme." *Growing Point*
ISBN 0-7445-1456-8   £2.99